The Merry-Mouse Schoolhouse

DOUBLEDAY & COMPANY, INC.
GARDEN CITY, NEW YORK

MERRY-
MOUSE
BOOK®

The Merry-Mouse Schoolhouse

PRISCILLA HILLMAN

Other Merry-Mouse books

A Merry-Mouse Christmas A-B-C
A Merry-Mouse Book of Months
A Merry-Mouse Book of Nursery Rhymes
A Merry-Mouse Book of Favorite Poems

Library of Congress Cataloging in Publication Data

Hillman, Priscilla.
   The merry-mouse schoolhouse.

   Summary: The three Nibble family children attend the
first day of school in the fall.
   [1. School stories.   2. Mice—Fiction]   I. Title.
PZ7.H5598Me   [E]   AACR2
ISBN: 0-385-17106-4   trade
        0-385-17107-2   prebound
Library of Congress Catalog Card Number 81-43137

To my dear friend Marie

Tucked snugly between the roots of a hollow oak tree lived a merry mouse family, the Nibbles. There were Mama and Papa Nibbles, Squeaky, and his two sisters, Muffy and Petunia.

The little mice had enjoyed a happy summer, swinging on the weeds and playing among the mushrooms that grew near their door. But now it was September. The leaves were turning color and were tumbling from the trees, the apples were red, and the pumpkins lay ripe and golden in the fields. Tomorrow the little red schoolhouse down the lane would be open once again.

The little mice went to bed early that night. In the morning the first rays of sunshine woke them. Squeaky and Petunia sat up and rubbed their eyes. They were happy to be returning to school today. And this year Muffy would be going with them.

"My first day of school," squeaked Muffy excitedly.

The three little mice dressed quickly and skipped down
the stairs to the kitchen, where Mama and Papa were
waiting for them. Mama Nibbles had prepared a platter of
fried crabapples and some creamy acorn porridge for
breakfast.

After eating for a while, Squeaky mumbled through a
mouthful of porridge, "I'm not hungry anymore, Mama."

"We're not, either," said Muffy and Petunia together as
they looked up at Mama Nibbles.

"Oh well," said Mama, "I guess you're too excited to eat very much this morning. Go wash up and get ready for school."

Squeaky, Petunia, and Muffy quickly washed their hands and faces in the wooden tub. Then the three merry mice scampered down the stairs to say good-bye to Mama and Papa.

Chattering excitedly, they gathered
up their school books and lunch.
Mama Nibbles, who was
standing by the door,
kissed each fondly and
waved good-bye.
"Be good," she said,
as they hurried into
the morning
sunshine.

It was a warm day, full of singing birds and ripe with
the smell of autumn.

Shuffling their feet through the carpet of golden leaves, Squeaky, Petunia, and Muffy hurried down the winding path.

"What is school like?" asked Muffy.

"You'll see," answered Petunia.

Squeaky ran ahead to join his friend, Chippy Chipmunk, who was kicking acorns as he walked along.

"Hi, Chippy," said Squeaky.

"We could have lots of fun, Squeaky, if we skipped school and kicked acorns instead," said Chippy hopefully.

"Not me," said Squeaky, as he kicked the acorn farther along the path. "I'm going to grow up and be a smart little mousie."

Soon they reached the little red schoolhouse. The teacher was standing by the door swinging the big bell back and forth to call the children into school.

"This is my sister, Muffy, and it's her first day of school," Petunia said proudly to the teacher.

"Well, well. I'm happy to meet you, Muffy," said the teacher, warmly, "I'm sure you are going to enjoy school."

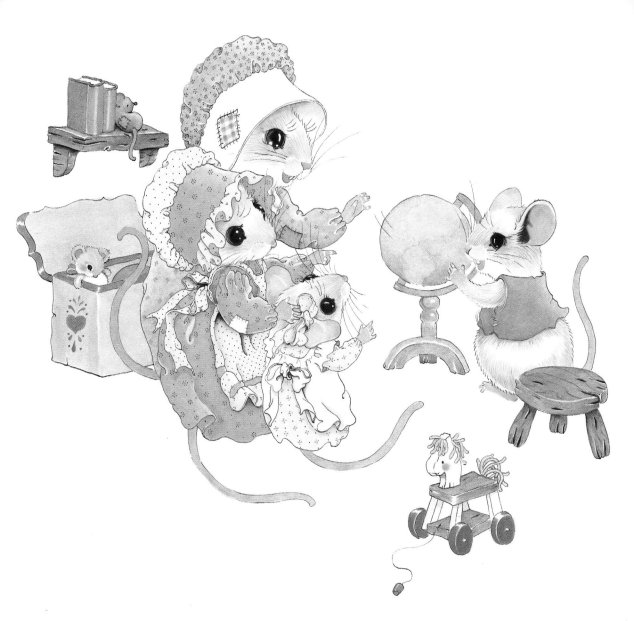

Petunia led Muffy inside, and Muffy looked around the cozy room. There were a large desk with a blackboard behind it, shelves of books, a chest full of toys, and all kinds of other interesting things.

"But what's that?" Muffy asked eagerly, as she pointed to a strange round object.

"This is a globe," shouted Squeaky, giving it a wild spin.

"Easy, Squeaky," the teacher said gently. "That's a globe of the earth, Muffy. That's where we live. You'll learn all about the earth soon."

"I'm happy to see you all here today,"
the teacher said, as the children
settled down on the old school bench.

Muffy excitedly clutched her apron as the teacher
explained some of the things they would learn.

"First, I'd like Muffy to learn her ABC's. Squeaky, help
her with the letter A, please," said the teacher, "while I
help Petunia with her addition."

The teacher turned to the blackboard and wrote
1 + 1 = . Petunia went to the board, thought a
moment, then picked up the chalk and wrote 2.

"Now, Squeaky," said the teacher, "I'd like you to
spell cat." Carefully, she wrote CAT on the blackboard
in large letters.

Squeaky carefully wrote CAT on his slate.
"I did it," he said.
"And I wrote A," murmured Muffy shyly.
"I'm proud of both of you," said the teacher, smiling
at them.

"Now it's time for art," said the teacher. "Petunia, you may paint on the easel in the back of the room, and the rest of you go to the art table. You'll find crayons and paper there."

Chippy, Muffy, and Squeaky rushed to the art table and began to draw.

"I'm drawing a picture of me," said Muffy as she bent over her paper.

"Look at my nice house," cried Squeaky, "and I drew the sun and a tree, too."

When they finished drawing, the teacher said, "You've all done such a good job, I think I'll read you a story before you go outside for lunch."

Then the teacher settled down in her chair with a book and Squeaky and Muffy huddled close beside her.

She is so nice, thought Muffy, as she looked up at the teacher.

Soon it was time for their lunch, and they went outside.
The three little mice found a good spot under a tree.
Petunia unwrapped a piece of cheese. Squeaky
sniffed the air deeply, wiggling his nose.
"I just love cheese," he said with delight.
"Of course you do, silly," laughed
Petunia, "you're a mouse."

After finishing their lunch, the little mice
played on the seesaw among the mushrooms,
while Chippy chattered down at them from his
perch on the swing.

"This is fun!" said Muffy happily, as the seesaw
went up and down.

In an hour the teacher rang the school bell, and
recess was over.

"Time for music!" said the teacher when they were all inside again. "There is an instrument for each of you on the cupboard shelf." She walked over to the old piano and sat down to play.

The children picked up their instruments and marched around the room, led by Squeaky, who was beating happily on the triangle.

When school was over, they all said good-bye to the
teacher and went skipping down the lane.

"I loved my first day of school," Muffy said.

"I knew you would," said Petunia.

"I like school, but I like to play outside, too," shouted Squeaky as he ran ahead to play in the dry leaves.

When they got home, they told their mother about all the exciting things they did at school.

"I drew a picture of me," said Muffy, as she held it up for Mama Nibbles to see.

"*I* can spell cat now," shouted Squeaky, hopping up and down.

"And I know that one and one are two," announced Petunia.

"How wonderful!" said Mama Nibbles. "I'm very proud of you. Now, go in and change and you may play until supper."

After supper, the little mice had their baths in the big wooden tub. Muffy had hers first and was soon dressed in her favorite nightgown.

"You're next, Squeaky," said Mama Nibbles.

"But I'm already clean," said Squeaky.

"Then, what is this sticky honey doing behind your ears?" Mama Nibbles said, laughing. "Into the tub, Squeaky, and use lots of soap."

"Squeaky doesn't like to wash," giggled Muffy from behind Mama Nibbles' apron.

Squeaky got into the tub slowly. Then he rubbed and scrubbed until his fur was sticking out in all directions and soap bubbles were spilling over the edges of the tub.

"Now, dry yourself well," said Mama Nibbles as she handed him a soft, fluffy towel.

Squeaky rubbed his fur until it was shiny and dry. "Now I'm clean as a whistle," he said.

Petunia was next.

When they were all washed and in their pajamas, they hurried over to Papa Nibbles, who was sitting in his overstuffed armchair. They snuggled around him and looked up hopefully.

"Will you read to us, Papa?" they asked.

Papa Nibbles often read them a story before bedtime.

"Yes, my dears," he said.

After polishing his glasses and putting them back on his nose, Papa Nibbles began to read. But, before he could finish, their eyes started to close drowsily.

"Bedtime, dears," Papa said softly.

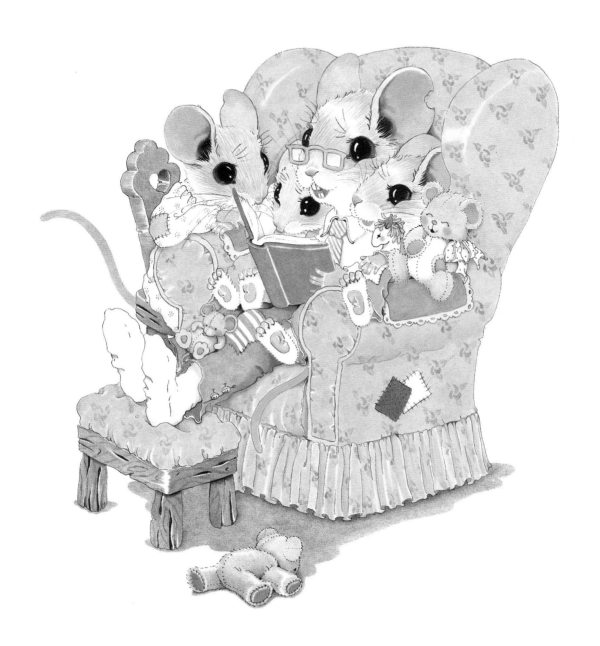

Squeaky yawned and hugged Papa Nibbles' stomach, which was nice and soft. Then he stumbled upstairs, followed closely by Muffy and Petunia.

They climbed into bed and snuggled down into the warm and comfy covers.

Mama and Papa came up and kissed them each warmly.

"Good night, little ones," they said as they turned out the light and tiptoed quietly out of the room. And soon, very soon, there were three merry mice fast asleep.